～ The Classic Tale of ～
Peter Rabbit

Manufactured in U.S.A.

8 7 6 5 4 3 2 1

ISBN 1-56173-474-8

Cover illustration by Anita Nelson

Book illustrations by Pat Schoonover

Once there were four little bunnies named Flopsy, Mopsy, Cottontail, and Peter. They lived with their mother under a big fir tree.

One sunny morning, Mother Rabbit told her little bunnies, "You may go out to play, but be sure to stay out of Mr. McGregor's garden. He does not like little rabbits and he will come chasing after you."

Flopsy, Mopsy, and Cottontail each took a basket, hoping to find some sweet wild blackberries. And Peter thought he looked rather fine in his new blue jacket with the shiny brass buttons.

"Run along, now," said Mother Rabbit. "I am going to the baker's." And off she went to buy a loaf of brown bread and five cinnamon buns.

Flopsy, Mopsy, and Cottontail were good little bunnies. They always listened to their mother. They went down the lane to look for blackberries.

But Peter was a naughty rabbit. He ran down the lane, through the fields, and squeezed under the gate to Mr. McGregor's garden! He could hardly wait to nibble some crunchy radishes and carrots.

First, Peter ate some lettuce and green beans. Then he ate some radishes. The carrots were delicious, but the onions were too strong for his taste. When Peter's tummy began to ache he went to look for some parsley.

But at the end of a garden row Peter saw Mr. McGregor. The farmer was on his hands and knees, planting young cabbages. When Mr. McGregor saw Peter Rabbit, he jumped up, grabbed his rake, and chased after the scared little bunny.

"Stop, thief!" shouted Mr. McGregor.

Peter was very frightened. He ran through the garden looking for the gate. Where was it? Peter knew he was lost.

Poor Peter lost one shoe among the cabbages and the other in the potato patch. Without his shoes he was able to run much faster. He might have gotten away, but the shiny brass buttons on his new blue jacket got tangled in a gooseberry net!

The only way Peter could get free of the net was to wriggle out of his new blue jacket and leave it behind.

Peter shed big tears. He was sure he would never find his way home.

Peter had no time to feel sorry for himself. Mr. McGregor was not far behind. Hop! Jump! Peter rushed into a tool shed and jumped inside a watering can. It would have been a good place to hide, had it not been half-full of water.

Mr. McGregor was sure Peter was hiding in the shed. Quietly and carefully he began turning over flower pots, looking under each one for the naughty little rabbit.

"Kertyschoo!" Peter sneezed. And Mr. McGregor was after him again.

Peter leaped out the window, upsetting three flower pots. Mr. McGregor tried to follow him, but the window was too small. And Mr. McGregor was tired of chasing the little rabbit. So he went back to his work in the garden.

Peter sat down to rest. He was shaking with fear and was out of breath. He did not know which way to go. He was also very damp from sitting in that watering can.

After a while, he began to wander around, going hippity-hop, not very fast. He looked around and saw a door in the wall, but it was locked.

Just then, a little mouse scampered past him. Peter asked her the way to the gate, but she had a large pea in her mouth and could not answer. She only shook her head at him. Peter began to cry again.

Peter wandered across the garden to a fish pond. There, a white cat sat very still, staring at the goldfish swimming in the pond. Peter had been warned about cats; he decided not to ask her the way to the gate.

Peter became more and more confused. He went back toward the tool shed. Suddenly, close to him, he heard the noise of a hoe—*scritch, scratch, scratch, scritch.*

Peter hid underneath some bushes. Nothing happened. So Peter climbed into a wheelbarrow for a better look around. The first thing he saw was Mr. McGregor hoeing onions. He had his back to Peter.

There it was! Just across the garden, beyond Mr. McGregor, was the gate! Peter ran to the gate as fast as he could and slid underneath it to safety. Mr. McGregor could not catch him now! Peter did not stop running until he reached his home beneath the big fir tree.

Mother Rabbit was busy cooking. Flopsy, Mopsy, and Cottontail were having a supper of bread, milk, and blackberries. Peter was too tired to eat. He flopped down on the soft sand floor and went to sleep.

Peter's mother tucked him into his bed and gave him a dose of camomile tea: "One tablespoonful to be taken at bedtime."

Mother Rabbit watched Peter sleep. She wondered where he had lost his little shoes and his new blue jacket with the shiny brass buttons.

Only Mr. McGregor knew where Peter's clothes were. He had hung them up like a scarecrow to frighten the blackbirds away from his garden.